For my hairbrush hater, Edith. Xxx

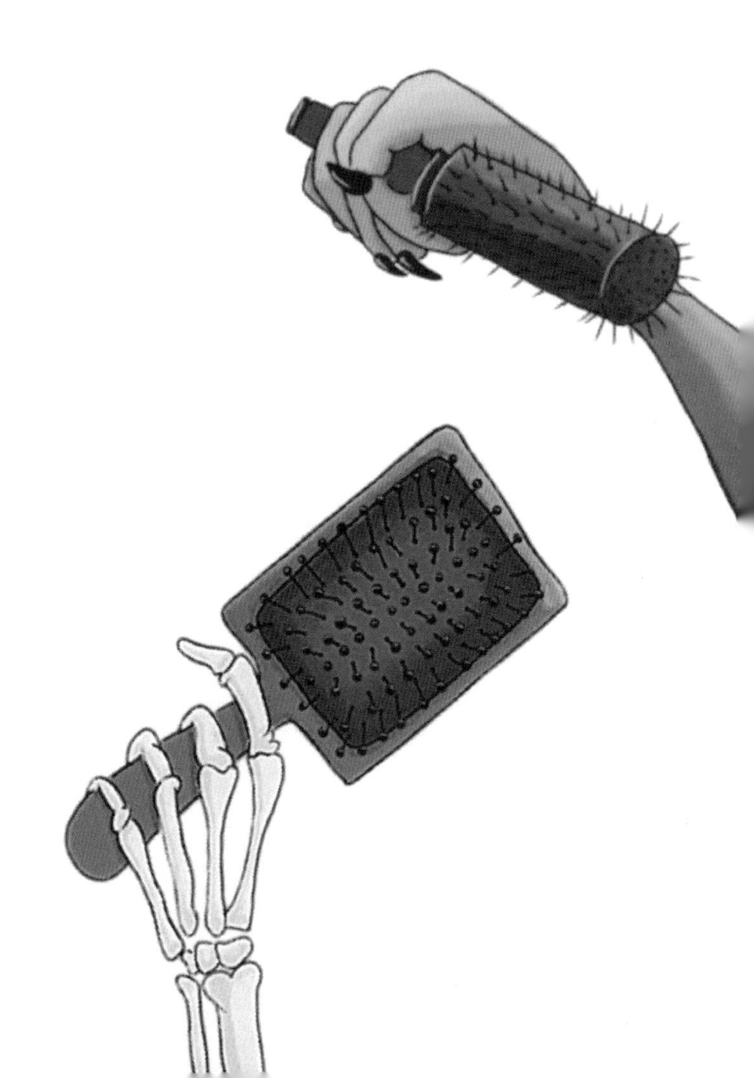

I wake up in the morning.

I get dressed and brush my teeth.

Then run straight to my bed, get down and hide right underneath!

The problem is my hair,

It's long and oh so very frizzy!

Just looking at that tangled mane,

It leaves me feeling dizzy!

I beg my Mum "Just cut it!" But she simply doesn't listen.
Each morning, in she creeps. I see the dreaded hairbrush glisten.

I'd say I'm pretty brave. In fact I'm much braver than most.

I wouldn't care a bit if I was haunted by a ghost!

I wouldn't mind, if from behind a monster loudly roared.

If skeletons jumped from my closet, frankly, I'd be bored.

I'd face a smelly swamp monster

All slimey, green and snotty,

But I cannot face the hairbrush,

When my hair is really knotty!

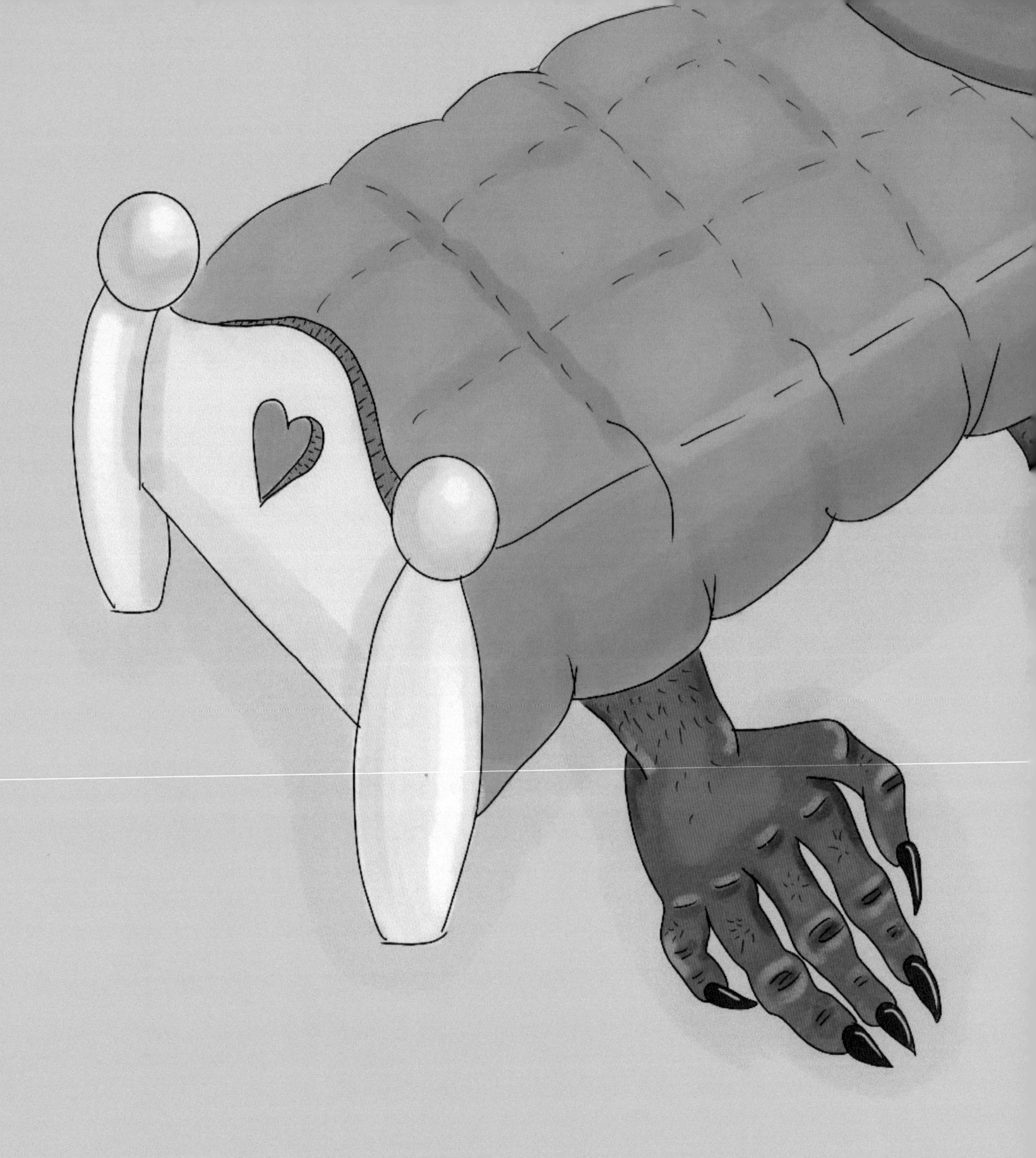

The Bogey Man under my bed
Would cause me little stress.

But I cannot face the hairbrush
When my hair is in a mess!

Abominable Snowman!?

I know I'd tame that Yeti.

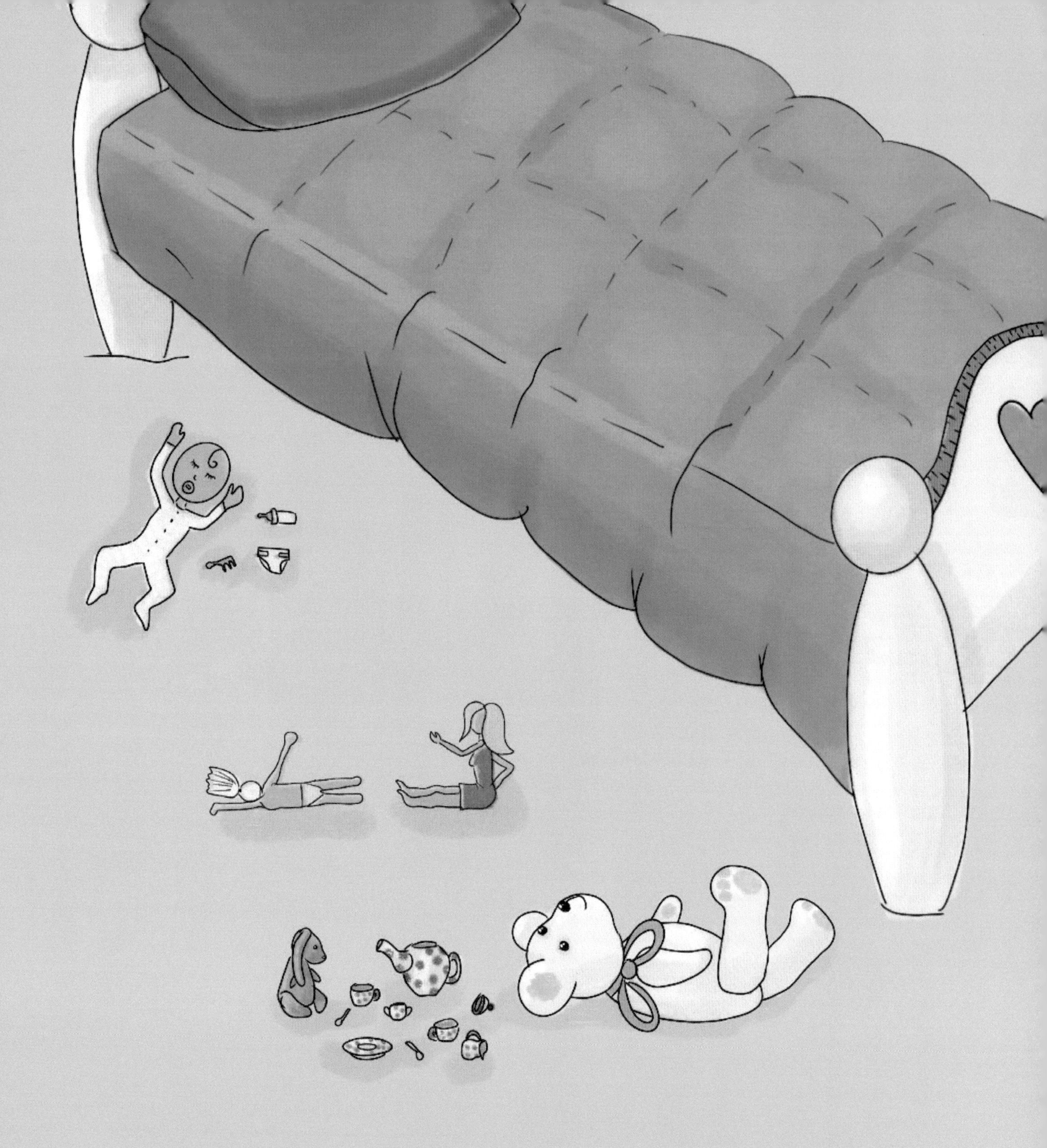

But I cannot face the hairbrush
When my hair looks like spaghetti!

I'd pet a giant spider from the ceiling where it dangled,
But I cannot face the hairbrush, when my hair has got all tangled!

Vampires flying through my window really wouldn't faze me.
But I cannot face the hairbrush when my hair has gone all crazy.

If Zombies lurched into my room,

I'd handle them, I dare say.

But I cannot face the hairbrush

When I'm having a bad hair day!

I'm Just Not Sleepy!
I'm Just Not Sleepy!

One day, I'm underneath my bed,
Hiding on the ground.
My wardrobe door starts opening,
A bony hand creeps round.

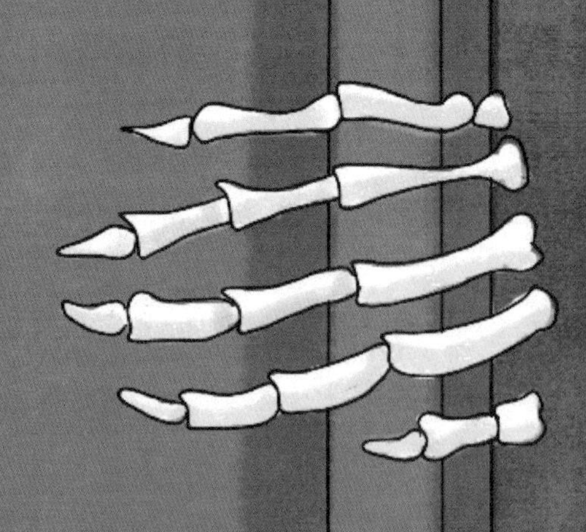

The curtains part and standing there,
A fearsome, grizzly sight.

Are seven Zombies, licking lips.

It's me they want to bite!

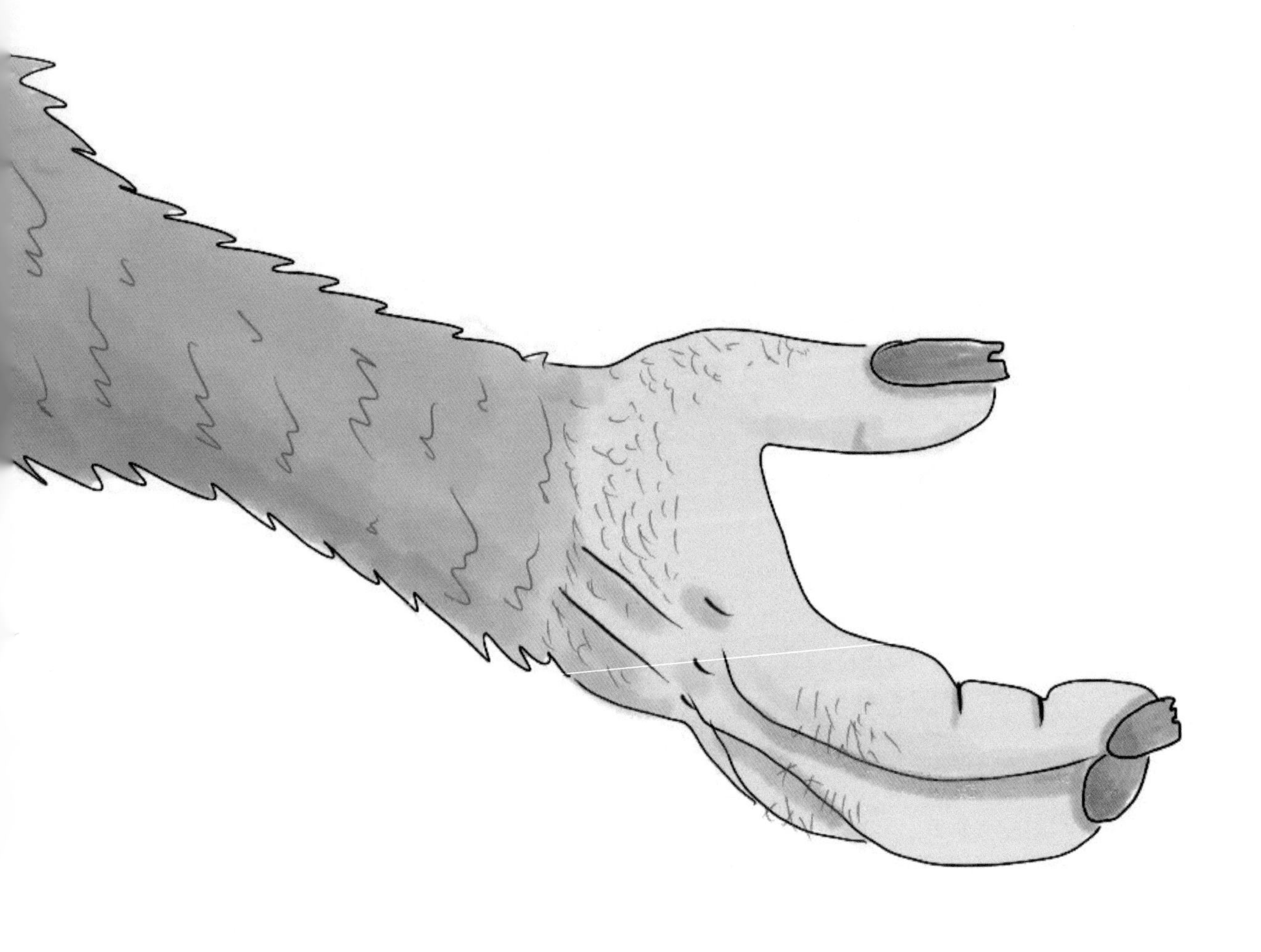

A hairy Yeti arm sweeps
underneath the bed to grab me.

Through my open window
flies a Vampire to nab me!

I look around and to my left,
The Bogeymans green eyes.
He gives an evil chuckle,
Just before he shouts "Surprise!"

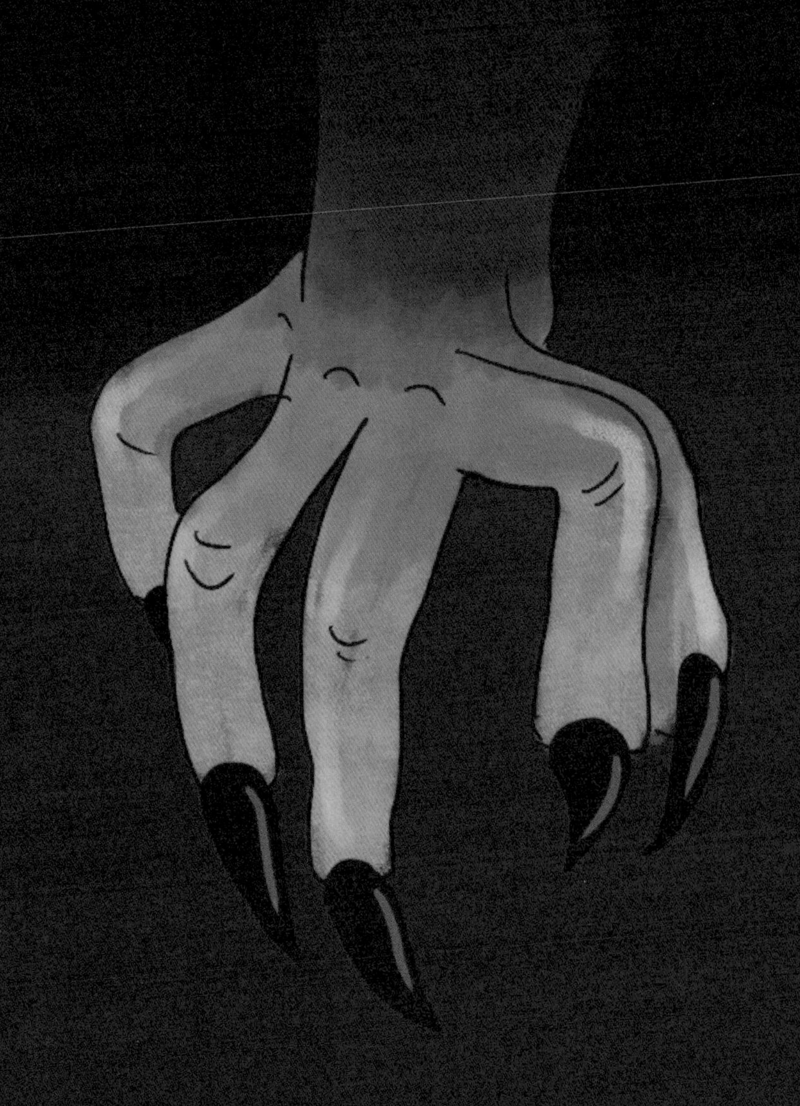

What shall I do? I wonder,
I'm not really very sure.
I hear the sound
of Mother's footsteps
coming on the floor.

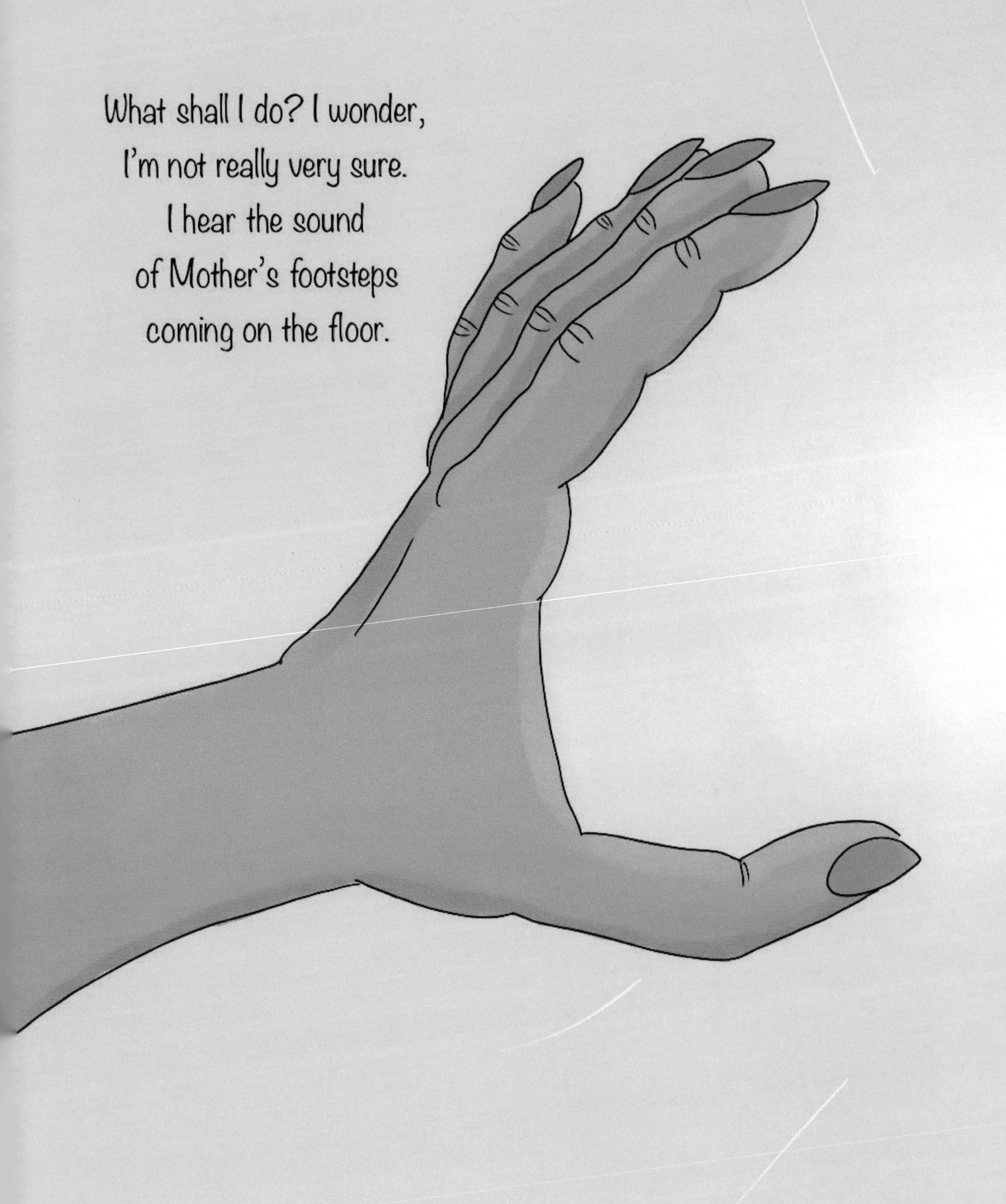

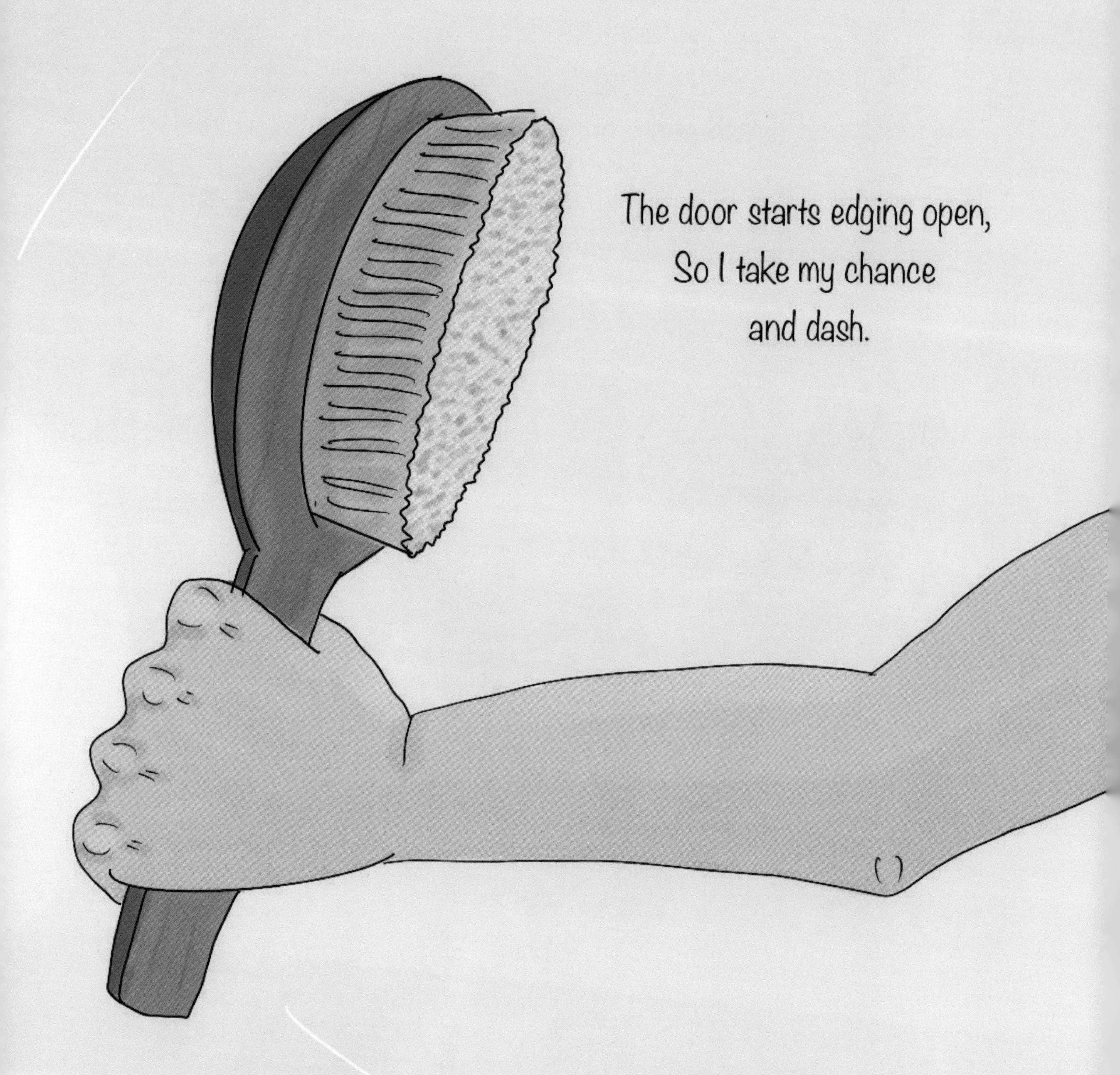

The door starts edging open,
So I take my chance
and dash.

I quickly grab the hairbrush
From Mum's hand and in a **flash**.....

The monsters all go flying
As I kick and thrash and prance.
Just like a proper Ninja,
All those beasts don't stand a chance!
KA-POW
BOOM!

My Mum's aghast! She's terrified!
She screams "Be careful dear!"
As one by one, those nasty, horrid
monsters disappear.

"You've saved my life!" Says Mum
"And it's a debt I can't repay."

I think for a few moments,
Then I answer "That's ok.
There is one thing that you can do to thank me."
I report.

"The only thing I want is for my hair to be cut short!"

So to the hairdressers we go,
And with a few quick snips;
My hair is gone and I can't keep the
smile from my lips!

My head feels cool and wonderful
And with a happy grin,
I jump for joy, I take the brush and throw
it in the bin!

Creepy cuts

Open
WELCOME
LITTER

So now, instead of tears each day,
Our house is filled with laughter.

And monster free, my Mum and me.....

Live happy ever after!

If you enjoyed this book, please consider leaving me a review!

If you really enjoyed the book, you might enjoy one of my other titles.

Visit www.Kidsbooks4nooks.com for free activity pages, information on upcoming projects and all my books.

Printed in Great Britain
by Amazon